To Sir Tomás
–R.A.–

To Sir Adam
–A.R.–

First edition for the United States and Canada published in 2007 by Barron's Educational Series, Inc.

First published in Great Britain in 2007 by
Orchard Books
338 Euston Road
London NW1 3BH

All inquiries should be addressed to:
Barron's Educational Series, Inc.
250 Wireless Boulevard
Hauppauge, NY 11788
http://www.barronseduc.com

Library of Congress Control Number: 2006937856

ISBN-13: 978-0-7641-6061-5
ISBN-10: 0-7641-6061-3

Printed in Singapore
9 8 7 6 5 4 3 2 1

Small Knight and George

Written by Ronda Armitage
Illustrated by Arthur Robins

BARRON'S

SMALL Knight lived in a cold, old castle on a spiky, high hill. He didn't mind that it was cold or old. He loved the castle so much that he never wanted to go anywhere else.

"DRAGONS live in caves, they breathe fire, and they're very fierce," explained Dad Knight. "You'll know one when you see one. Knights have to be big and brave and fight them. That's what knights do."

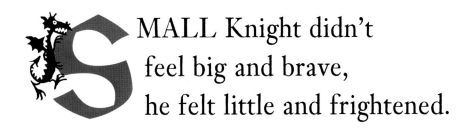MALL Knight didn't feel big and brave, he felt little and frightened.

He clunked in his armor and shivered in his boots, and made up a song as he rode along:

"This is a tale of
a big brave knight

Who one fine day
went out to fight

A very fierce dragon
who lived in a cave."

S OON Small Knight
came to a hut.
He tapped on the door.
"I'm looking for a very fierce
dragon," he said politely.
"Have you seen one about?"

"Don't talk to me about
fierce dragons," said Mr. Peasant.
"One knocked the roof off my
hut with a swipe of its scaly tail.
Are you sure you want to fight
a very fierce dragon?"
"It's what brave knights do,"
explained Small Knight.

But he looked at the hut
and he didn't feel brave.

MALL Knight came to a village. Six damsels were combing their golden hair. "Excuse me," called Small Knight. "I'm looking for a very fierce dragon. Have you seen one about?"

DISTRESS
1

"Don't talk to us about fierce dragons," cried the six damsels. "One roared down the street this morning. He gave us such a fright he made our hair stand on end. Are you sure you want to fight a very fierce dragon?"
"It's what brave knights do," explained Small Knight.

But he gazed at their hair and he didn't feel brave.

SMALL Knight came to a forest. A woodcutter was sitting on a tree trunk. "Good afternoon," said Small Knight. "I'm looking for a very fierce dragon. Have you seen one about?"

"Don't talk to me about fierce dragons," groaned the woodcutter. "One breathed fire and burned the forest down. Are you sure you want to fight a very fierce dragon?" "It's what brave knights do," explained Small Knight.

But he looked at the trees and he didn't feel brave.

SMALL Knight clunked in his armor and shivered in his boots. He sang a different song as he rode along:

"This is a song of
a not-so-brave knight

Who decided one day
he didn't want to fight

A very fierce dragon
who lived in a cave."

O N the way home he found a little creature. "Good evening," said Small Knight. "I'm Small Knight, and I'm *supposed* to be looking for a very fierce dragon. Have you seen one about?"

"Don't talk to me about fierce dragons," cried the little creature. "I used to have a lovely dark home in a hill, but some very fierce dragons moved in, and now I have no home. Are you sure you want to fight a very fierce dragon?"

"OT now," said Small Knight. "It's getting dark. I'll look for a very fierce dragon tomorrow. Please don't cry. You can stay at my home tonight."

"Thank you, Small Knight," sniffled the little creature. "Please call me George."

So, Small Knight and George hurried home.

Mrs. Knight was waiting at the castle gate.

"Hello, Mom," called Small Knight. "I've brought my new friend home to stay."

MOM Knight and the ladies-in-waiting ran screaming to the ramparts. Dad Knight and the knights scrambled up to the Minstrels' Gallery.

"Mom, Dad," called Small Knight. "I've been looking for dragons to fight all day and now it's time for tea."

"You only had to fight the very fierce dragon..." called Mom Knight, "You didn't have to bring him home!"

"Where?"

said Small Knight.

"There!"

cried everybody.

"Get behind me, George," shouted Small Knight. "There's a very fierce dragon about. I'm a big brave knight; I'll look after you."

"Excuse me, Small Knight," said George. "I think there's been a mistake. I'm the dragon."
"But dragons are big and fierce and breathe fire," said Small Knight. "I'm a friendly, gentle sort of dragon," smiled George. "I'm frightened of fierce dragons too."

"A dragon," cheered Small Knight. "A real dragon. Could you pretend to be very fierce so I can fight you?"

NEXT morning, they had a wonderful fight where no one won at all, and they played kickball for the rest of the day.

Everybody
loved
George.

He showed all of the knights the best way to fight very fierce dragons, and he learned how to breathe fire to keep that cold, old castle warm . . .